Bathtub Blues

by **Kate McMullan**

Illustrated by

Janie Bynum

LITTLE, BROWN AND COMPANY

New York · Boston

For the newest rocker, Amelia Elizabeth Owen

— K. M.

For Kayla, who loved her Dirty Baby.

— J. B.

Text copyright © 2005 by Kate McMullan
Illustrations copyright © 2005 by Janie Bynum
Music by Paul Hodes, copyright © 2005 by Big Round Music, LLC
"Bathtub Blues" performed by Peggo and Paul with the Peggosus Band
℗ 2005 by Big Round Music, LLC

Little, Brown and Company

Time Warner Book Group
1271 Avenue of the Americas, New York, NY 10020
Visit our Web site at www.lb-kids.com

First Edition

Library of Congress Cataloging-in-Publication Data
McMullan, Kate.
Bathtub blues / by Kate McMullan ; illustrated by Janie Bynum.— 1st ed.
p. cm.
Summary: Ten stinky members of the Rock-a-Baby Band sing and play while taking a bath.
ISBN 0-316-60901-3
[1. Babies—Fiction. 2. Baths—Fiction. 3. Music—Fiction. 4. Stories in rhyme.] I. Bynum, Janie, ill.
II. Title.
PZ8.3.M238Bat 2005
[E]—dc22   2003022687

10 9 8 7 6 5 4 3 2 1

IM

Manufactured in China

The illustrations for this book were done in digital gouache.
The text was set in Kidprint, and the display type was hand-lettered by Janie Bynum.

One baby, two baby,
three baby, four,
Charlotte, Denny,
Bip, and Ling
running out the door.

Rock-a-Baby rockers
are back to play again!

Oh, sandy, sandy, sandy,
babies need a scrub.
All you sandy babies
jump into the tub!

Charlotte does a puddle dance,
spatters Denny's shirt,

Bip and Ling plop down and sing:
"Babies, dig that dirt!"

Charlotte hugs her big wet dog,

Denny spills his drink,

Oh, stinky, stinky, stinky,
babies need a scrub.
All you stinky babies
jump into the tub!

One baby, two baby, three baby, four,
howling in the bathtub—here come some more
Five, six, seven, eight, all of them in tears,
nine, ten rockers screaming.

"We've got the bathtub blues,
we've got 'em bad, so, so bad."

"A little dirt?
What can it hurt?
We've got the
bathtub blues."

Charlotte finds a rubber duck,

Denny nabs a cup,

Bip and Ling grab EVERYthing!
Bath time's looking up.

Oh, splashy, splashy, splashy,
babies whoop and shout.
"Bath time's over, Babies,"
everybody, out!

One baby, two baby, three baby, four,
Charlotte, Denny, Bip, and Ling heading for the door,
Five baby, six baby, seven, eight, nine, ten!